The Wales that inspired

Dylan Thomas

Photographs by Brian Gaylor

The Wales that inspired Dylan Thomas
Return Journey to the Welsh World of Dylan Thomas

Words by Dylan Thomas
Photography by
Brian Gaylor. FRPS, BA(Hons)

Design & Typeset by
Mass Media Digital Ltd, Swansea
in Elegant Garamond Italic 10pt

Printed by
DWJones (Printers) Ltd, Port Talbot.

Bookbinding by
Principal Bookbinders, Ystradgynlais.

First Edition Published 2003
Tŷ Llŷn Publications, City & County of Swansea
in association with
Octopws.co.uk

ISBN 0-95338-654-4-6

www.dylanthomas.org.
www.photosofwales.co.uk

FOREWORD

BY AERONWY THOMAS

Brian Gaylor's photographs present visual images drawn from the poetry and prose of Dylan Thomas. The written works that inspired them were published from the 1930s up to the early 1950s, and although my father was writing about these places and people fifty years ago, Gaylor has picked out the timeless images of leafy woods and restless seas.

Gaylor has not restricted himself to the poems and stories which portray Swansea and the other sea towns of south west Wales. My father's letters have also been sourced for their visual imagery, rich in poetic metaphor as might be expected but firmly anchored in real places that still exist. My father often bases his work on his own life experiences and the locations where they took place.

What gives this collection of photographs such vitality is Gaylor's appreciation of my father's zest for life in which nature in all its moods is paramount, though without excluding its inhabitants: animal and human. The poems which describe in lyrical terms the landscape, sea and rivers of Wales, are simply illustrated in the photographs as Gaylor's photographic eye selects elements from these same locations. Gaylor has his own artistic and personal vision of my father's work, and has exerted his rights as maker of the photographic image to visually represent his response to the characters from the plays and stories my father wrote.

Every photograph has an evocative quotation. The first one I turn to is typical: a moody picture of driftwood in what looks like water, with a reflection of leafy branches. The effect of the broken branch floating mistily in reflected water is both aesthetically pleasing and challenging to the eye and thought. Underneath are the words from a lesser known poem:

> For I shall turn the strongest stomach up
> With filth I gather
> From the thousand minds, all lust and wind
> Like a beachcomer in a time of light.

In this way, the artful photographer has selected and linked an image with words, with word and image each in their own way lend new interest to the other. I have found by looking at this particular image linked with words intriguing and stimulating, prompting me to return to the original poem to read it in its entirety, my interest re-generated by Gaylor's densely rich image and his choice of related words to illustrate it.

Each photograph and accompanying text offers the same stimulation: a visual image that can act as an introductory pathway to some of Dylan's greatest and lesser known works. I am confident that this book will surely be a useful tool to introduce my father's work to a new audience and develop the interest of those already familiar with his varied output. Personally, after nearly fifty years studying my father's work, I find a new impetus in this exceptional photographic collection to re-examine and enjoy the words and works from which the images took inspiration.

DYLAN THOMAS' WALES: IMAGES OF INSPIRATION

INTRODUCTION

This project started life two and a half years ago as a CD, intended as a keepsake for visitors to the Dylan Thomas Centre's 'Man and Myth' exhibition. However, as Brian's knowledge of, and passion for, the work of Dylan Thomas grew, this project and our collaboration developed to the extent that it was clear that a simple CD would not suffice.

Having spent a considerable time reading, re-reading and absorbing a wide range of Dylan's poetry and prose, Brian travelled throughout south and west Wales with his digital camera placing Dylan's works in a modern visual context. The images illuminate the words on the page, and the words can also help explain the photographs.

This book is intended to be both educational and inspirational, making Dylan's work accessible to those unfamiliar with it, whilst encouraging people who are already fans to re-read Dylan with renewed enthusiasm. Such is the variety of work selected by Brian that even those steeped in Dylan's writing should find a quote they have not read before, or cannot remember reading, and will return once again to the great man's works.

Sean Keir
Cultural Development Officer,
City and County of Swansea

The Wales that inspired

Dylan Thomas

I, in my intricate image, stride on two levels,
Forged in man's minerals, the brassy orator
Laying my ghost in metal,

...My images stalk the trees and the slant sap's tunnel,
No tread more perilous, the green steps and spire
Mount on man's footfall,

To begin at the beginning

I first saw the light of day in a Glamorgan villa, and amid the terrors of the Welsh accent and the smoke of the tin plate stacks

...an ugly, lovely town ...crawling, sprawling, ...by the side of a long and splendid curving shore ...This sea-town was my world

...over the yellow seashore, and the stone-chasing dogs and the old men and the singing sea beyond that unknown Wales with its wild names like peals of bells in the darkness

Though it was only a little park, it held within its
borders of old tall trees notched with our names and
shabby from our climbing as many secret places
caverns and forests, prairies and deserts, as a country
somewhere at the end of the sea.

*...I discovered new refuges and
ambushes in its miniature
woods and jungles,
hidden homes and lairs,*

*...for the multitude of the young,
for cowboys and Indians...
full of terrors and treasures...*

The hunchback in the park
A solitary mister
Propped between trees and water
From the opening of the garden lock
That lets the trees and water enter
Until the Sunday-sombre bell at dark

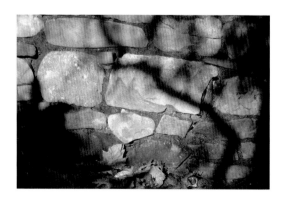

All night in the unmade park
After the railings and shrubberies
The birds the grass the trees and the lake
And the wild boys innocent as strawberries
Had followed the hunchback
To his kennel in the dark.

over the trees of the eternal Park,
where a brass band shakes the leaves
and sends them showering down on to
the nurses and the children, the cripples
and the out-of-work.

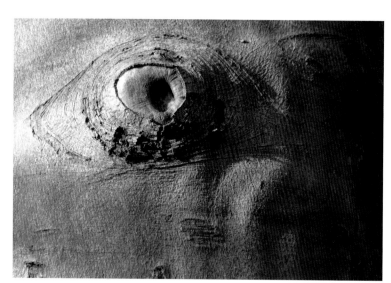

...and, most sinister of all, the far off race
of the Mormons, a people who every night
rode on nightmares through my bedroom.

...I used to dawdle on half-holidays along the bent and Devon-facing seashore hoping for corpses or gold watches or the skull of a sheep or a message in a bottle to be washed up in the wreck.

the lonely schoolroom where only the sometimes tearful
wicked sat over undone sums or to repent a little crime

...the gaunt pier, there to clamber under the pier, hanging
perilously on its skeleton-legs

...for the Park, the inexhaustibly ridiculous and mysterious... where the hunchback sat alone, images of perfection in his head,

The recollections of childhood have no order; of all those every-coloured and shifting scented shoals that move below the surface of the moment of recollection.

Poetry (the Spinster's Friend) first unveiled herself to me when I was six or seven years old: she still remains, though sometimes her face is cracked across like an old saucer.

The first ten years in school and park
Leapt like a ball from light to dark,
Bogies scared from landing and from corner,

...The next five years from morn to even
Hung between hell and heaven.
Plumbed devil's depths, reached angel's heights;
Dreams would have tempted saints at nights;

One afternoon, in a particularly bright and glowing
August, some years before I knew I was happy,

...When we reached Mewslade Beach and flung ourselves down,
as I scooped up sand and it trickled, grain by grain through my
fingers,
...knowing always that the sea dashed on the rocks not far below
us and rolled out into the world...

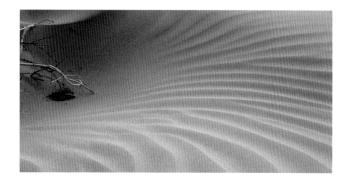

And this is true, no man can live
Who does not bury god in a deep grave
And then raise up the skeleton again,

There is one bay almost too lovely to look at. You shall come and see it
with me; we shall both utter words of maudlin wonder, and swoon
away on the blasted heath

For I shall turn the strongest stomach up
With filth I gather
From the thousand minds, all lust and wind
Like a beachcomber in the time of light

Let me escape,
Be free (wind for my tree and water for my flower),
Live self for self,
And drown the gods in me

I'll cut through your dark cloud
To see the sun myself,
Pale and decayed, an ugly growth.

All reason broke, and horror walked the roads.
A smile let loose a devil, a bell struck.
He could hear women breathing in the dark,

Awake, my sleeper, to the sun,
A worker in the morning town,
And leave the poppied pickthank where he lies;
The fences of the light are down,
All but the briskest riders thrown,
And worlds hang on the trees.

My purple is turning, I think, into a dull grey. I am at the most transitional period now.

It was as if the night was crying, crying out the terrible explanation of itself. On all sides of me, under my feet, above my head, the symbols moved, all waiting in vain to be translated. The trees that night were like prophets' fingers.

The passage grew dark too suddenly, the walls crowded in, and the roofs crouched down.

I remember the demon in the story, with his wings and hooks, who clung like a bat to my hair as I battled up and down Wales.

...the farm-yard of Gorsehill, where the cobbles rang and the black, empty stables took up the ringing and hollowed it so that we drew up in a hollow circle of darkness...

I climbed the stairs; each had a different voice.
The house smelt of rotten wood and damp and animals.
I thought I had been walking long damp passages all my life.

There was nowhere like that farm-yard in all the slapdash county,
nowhere so poor and grand and dirty

...casting an ebony shadow, with the Gorsehill jungle swarming,
the violent, impossible birds and fishes leaping, hidden under
four-stemmed flowers the height of horses...in a dingle near Carmarthen

The odour of death stinks...I have rarely encountered it...
and find it rather pleasant.

It lends a little welcome melodrama to the drawing-room
tragi-comedy of my most uneventful life.

Now could I raise
Her dead, dark body to my own
And hear the joyous rustle of her bone
And in her eyes see deathly blaze;

Of tides that never touch the shores.
I *who was rich was made the richer*
By *sipping at the vine of days.*

I, *born of flesh and ghost, was neither*
A *ghost nor man, but mortal ghost.*
And *I was struck down by death's feather.*
I *was mortal to the last*

*...where the small and hardly known and the
never-to-be-forgotten people of the dirty town
had lived and loved and died, and, always, lost...*

*to write anything, just to let the words and ideas, the half
remembered half forgotten images, tumble on the sheets of paper.*

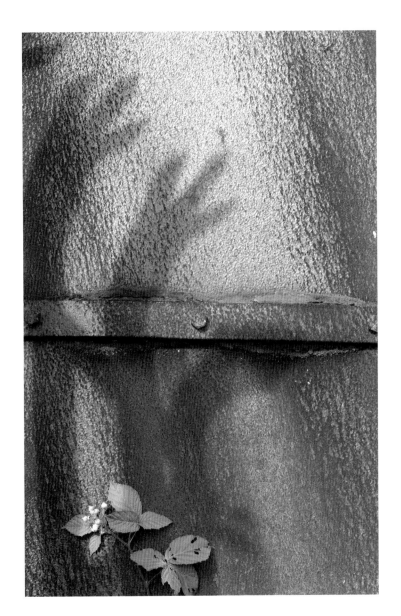

I see you boys of summer in your ruin.
Man in his maggot's barren.
And boys are full and foreign in the pouch.
I am the man your father was.
We are the sons of flint and pitch.
O see the poles are kissing as they cross.

That sanity be kept I sit at open windows,
Regard the sky, make unobtrusive comments on the moon,
Sit at open windows in my shirt,

...For sanity must be preserved,
Thinking of death, I sit and watch the park

The force that through the green fuse drives the flower
Drives my green age; that blasts the roots of trees
Is my destroyer.
And I am dumb to tell the crooked rose
My youth is bent by the same wintry fever.

*What was Christ in us was stuck with a bayonet to the sky, and
what was Judas we fed and sheltered, rewarding at the end,
with thirty hanks of flesh*

Especially when the October wind
With frosty fingers punishes my hair,
Caught by the crabbing sun I walk on fire
And cast a shadow crab upon the land,
By the sea's side, hearing the noise of birds,

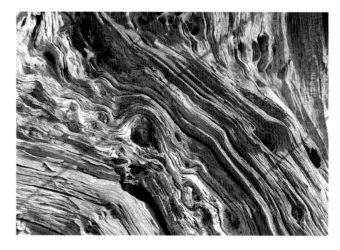

When, like a running grave, time tracks you down,
Your calm and cuddled is a scythe of hairs,
Love in her gear is slowly through the house,
Up naked stairs, a turtle in a hearse,
Hauled to the dome,

Deliver me, my masters, head and heart,
Heart of Cadaver's candle waxes thin,

I have longed to move away but am afraid;
Some life, yet unspent, might explode
Out of the old lie burning on the ground,
And crackling into the air, leave me half-blind.

The best in a man comes
out in suffering, there is a
prophet in pain, and an
oracle in the agony of the
mind...Death to me is no
more than going into
another room.

The voices of fourteen years ago hung
silent in the snow and ruin, and in the
falling winter morning I walked...

Yes, I remember him well, the boy you are
searching for:...he cribbed, mitched, spilt ink,
rattled his desk and garbled his lessons
with the best of them.

The names of the dead in the living heart and head remain for ever. Of all the dead whom did he know?

Oh yes, yes, I remember him well...He'd mooch about the dunes and watch the tankers and tugs and the banana boats come out of the docks. ...He was going to run away to sea, he said.

...Oh yes, I knew him well. I think he was happy all the time. I've known him by the thousands.

Ears in the turrets hear
Hands grumble on the door,
Eyes in the gables see
The fingers at the locks.
Shall I unbolt or stay
Alone until the day I die
Unseen by stranger -eyes
In this white house?
Hands, hold you poison or grapes?

I was the boy in a dream, and I stood stock still, knowing that the voice was mine and the dark was not the death of the sun.

I woke up in death, but there I forgot the dream and moved into a different being in the image of the boy who was terrified of the dark.

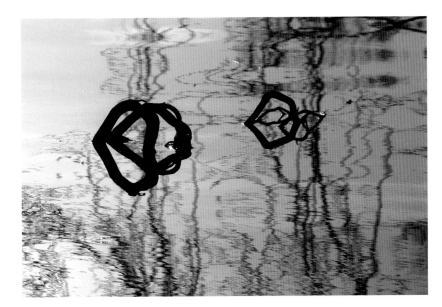

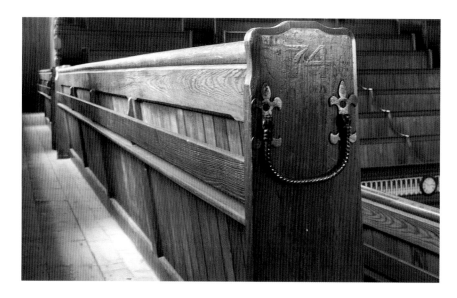

...the corpses of strangled preachers, promising
all their days a heaven
they don't believe in to people who won't go
there, float and hide truth.

The hand that signed the paper felled a city;
Five sovereign fingers taxed the breath,
Doubled the globe of dead and halved a country;
These five kings did a king to death.

Thank God it's dark. Now I can't see the people outside. I might be in a world of my own, owing nothing but the seeds of hate to all the dark passers scuttling to...stinking churches.

Altarwise by owl-light in the halfway-house
The gentleman lay gravewards with his furies;

...Bit out the mandrake with tomorrow's scream.
Then, penny-eyed, that gentleman of wounds,
Old cock from nowheres and the heaven's egg,
With bones unbuttoned to the halfway winds,

...life has no pattern and no purpose, but that a twisted
vein of evil, like the poison in a drinker's glass, coils up
from the pit to the top of the hemlocked world

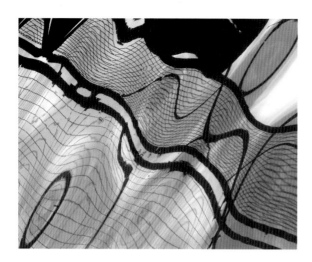

The seed-at-zero shall not storm
That town of ghosts, the trodden womb
With her rampart to his tapping,
No god-in-hero tumble down
Like a tower on the town
Dumbly and divinely stumbling
Over the manwaging line.

The tombstone told when she died.
Her two surnames stopped me still.
A virgin married at rest.

...Before she lay on a stranger's bed
With hand plunged through her hair,
Or that rainy tongue beat back

...She cried her white-dressed limbs were bare
And her red lips were kissed black,
She wept in her pain and made mouths,

The bay is one of the wildest, bleakest and barrenest I know-four or five miles of yellow coldness going away into the distance of the sea.

...And the worm ...a seaworm of rock pointing into the channel, is the very promontory of depression.

...spend the afternoon walking alone over the very desolate Gower Cliffs, communing with the cold and bitterness, I call this taking my devils for an airing

I still sedulously pluck the flowers of alcohol,
and, occasionally, but not as often as I wish,
am pricked by the drunken thorn.

And death shall have no dominion.
Dead men naked they shall be one
With the man in the wind and the west moon;
When their bones are picked clean and the clean bones gone,
They shall have stars at elbow and foot;

It is the sinners' dust-tongued bell claps me to churches
When, with his torch and hourglass, like a sulphur priest,
His beast heel cleft in a sandal,
Time marks a black aisle kindle from the brand of ashes,
Grief with dishevelled hands tear out the altar ghost
And a firewind kill the candle.

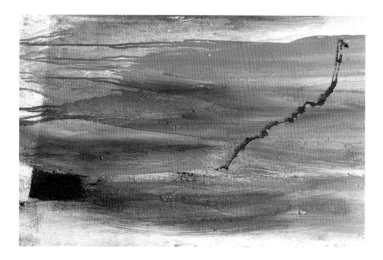

I know her scrubbed and sour humble hands
Lie with religion in their cramp, her threadbare
Whisper in a damp word, her wits drilled hollow,
Her fist of a face died clenched on a round pain;

My own news is very big and simple.
I was married three days ago;

My wife is Irish and French
...has seas of golden hair
...two dancing legs, is untidy and vague

And out of sleep, where the moon had raised him
through the mountains in her eyes
...called his furies by their names from the wind
drawn index of grave and water.

Should lanterns shine, the holy face,
Caught in an octagon of unaccustomed
light,
Would wither up, and any boy of love
Look twice before he fell from grace.

I have heard many years of telling,
And many years should see some change.

The ball I threw while playing in the park
Has not yet reached the ground.

I, in my intricate image, stride on two levels,
Forged in man's minerals, the brassy orator
Laying my ghost in metal,

...My images stalk the trees and the slant sap's tunnel,
No tread more perilous, the green steps and spire
Mount on man's footfall,

The dark struggling world
with its riches, hostilities,
bitches, unjustices, obscene
middle age, is a tastless joke...

...a terror of fearful expectation, a discovery and facing of fear. I hold a beast,
an angel, and a madman in me, and my enquiry is as to their working,

We who are young are old, and unbelieving,
Sit at our hearths from morning until evening,
Warming dry hands and listening to the air;
We have no faith to set between our teeth.
Believe, believe and be saved, we cry, who have no faith.

A grief ago,
She who was who I hold, the fats and flower,
Or, water-lammed, from the scythe-sided thorn,
Hell wind and sea,
A stem cementing, wrestled up the tower,
Rose maid and male,
Or, masted venus, through the paddler's bowl
Sailed up the sun;

My image, principally, did
not make the grave a gentle
cultivator but a tough
possessor, a warring and
complicated raper...

The afternoon was dying; lazily, namelessly drifting westward through the insects in the shade; over hill and tree and river and corn and grass to the evening shaping in the sea.

There was a story once upon a time whispered in the water voice; it blew out of the echo from the trees behind the beach in the golden hollows scraped on the wood until the musical birds and beasts came jumping into sunshine.

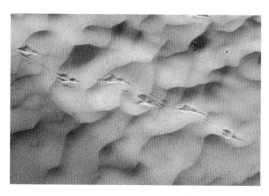

The piece of a wind in the sun was like the wind in an empty house; it made the corners mountains and crowded the attics with shadows who broke through the roof; through the country corridors it raced in a hundred voices, each voice larger than the last, until the last voice tumbled down and the house was full of whispers.

And some, like myself, just came, one day, for the day, and never left; got off the bus, and forgot to get on again.

How shall my animal
Whose wizard shape I trace in the cavernous skull,

...Endure burial under the spelling wall,

I *warn you that our cottage is pokey and ugly, four rooms like stained boxes in a workman's and fisherman's row, with a garden leading down to mud and sea,*

...a small damp fisherman's furnished cottage-green rot sprouts through the florid scarlet forests of the wallpaper, sneeze and the chairs crack, the double-bed is a swing band with coffin,

...cut out that remark of mine about ' I have a beast and an angel in me' or whatever it was: it makes me sick, drives me away from drink, recalls too much the worst of the fat and curly boy I know too well,

'See', drummed the taut masks, 'how the dead ascends: In the groin's endless coil a man is tangled.'

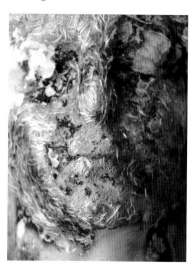

The stocked heart is forced, and agony has another mouth to feed.

O wake to see, after a noble fall,

The breath draw back like a bolt through white oil And a stranger enter like iron.

We've moved house & tilted our noses. Our previous house, once a palace, is now that cottage. How we ever existed there is beyond us. Here we could have two bedrooms each, which is quite useless.

In the poles of the year
When black birds died like priests in the cloaked hedge row
And over the cloth of counties the far hills rode near,
Under the one leaved trees ran a scarecrow of snow
And fast through the drifts of the thickets antlered like deer

... for I'm deep in money troubles,
small for some, big as banks for me,
my debts are raising, it's raining, my new
troubles and poems won't move,
what have I got to sparkle about...

On no work of words now for three lean months in the bloody
Belly of the rich year and the big purse of my body
I bitterly take to task my poverty and craft:

...To surrender now is to pay the expensive ogre twice.
Ancient woods of my blood, dash down to the nut of the seas
If I take to burn or return this world which is each man's work.

Girls hot and stupid for soldiers flock knickerless on the cliff. We're returning to Laugharne tomorrow. There are only 50 soldiers there. What are you doing for your country? I'm letting mine rot.

...the armed forces are not conducive to the creation of contemplative verse, and that all my few sources of income are drying up as quickly as blood on the Western Front.

*In the middle of the night I woke
from a dream full of whips and
lariats as long as serpents...
and wide, windy gallops over
cactus fields,*

*...late on my last morning, out of dreams where the Llanstephan
sea carried bright sailing-boats as long as liners;*

*Grandpa said: 'I am going to Llangadock to be buried.'
...then: 'there's no sense in lying dead in Llanstephan,'
...like a prophet who has no doubt.*

There was a saviour
Rarer than radium,
Commoner than water, crueller than truth;
Children kept from the sun
Assembled at his tongue
To hear the golden note turn in a groove,
Prisoners of wishes locked their eyes
In the jails and studies of his keyless smiles

I miss the boys and the smoky nights.
Here everything is so slow and prettily sad.
I'd like to live in a town or city again for a bit

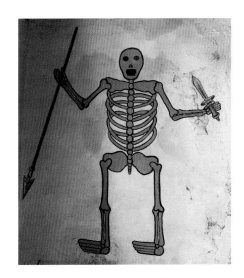

What have we got to fight for or against?
To prevent Facism coming here?
It's come ...But temptation's not too strong,
and sanity of the imagination is.

In my craft or sullen art
Excercised in the still night
When only the moon rages
And the lovers lie abed
With all their griefs in their arms,
I labour by singing light
Not for ambition or bread
Or the strut and trade of charms

A stranger has come
To share my room in the house not right in the head,
A girl mad as birds

Bolting the night of the door with her arm her plume.
Strait in the mazed bed
She deludes the heaven-proof house with entering clouds

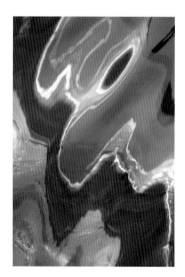

Woe drip from the dishrag hands and
the pressed sponge of the forehead,

Where at night we stoned the cold and cuckoo
Lovers in the dirt of their leafy beds,
The shade of their trees was a word of many shades
And a lamp of lightning for the poor in the dark;

...we walked on under the afternoon sun, growing thirsty and drowsy but never slowing our pace. Soon the cycling party rode by...all laughing and ringing.

...and saw grey chapels and weather-worn angels; at the feet of the hills farthest from the sea, pretty pink cottages- horrible I thought,

The sun was nearly right down...the sea began to cover our rock quickly, our rock already covered with friends, with living and dead, racing against the darkness.

And one man's year is like the country of a cloud, mapped on the sky, that soon will vanish into the watery, ordered wastes, into the spinning rule, into the dark which is light.

The crisp path through the field in this December snow, in the deep dark, where we trod the buried grass like ghosts on dry toast.

And then the moment of a night in that cavorting spring, rare and unforgettable as a bicycle-clip found in the middle of the desert.

With my red veins full of money,
In the final direction of the elementary town
I advance for as long as forever is.

Man is denying his partner man or woman
and whores with the whole night, begetting
a monstrous brood;

...in the deep woods ouside the villages in the
gulleys of the bare mountains, by lamplight
in the caves we had known as boys

Into her lying down head
His enemies entered bed,
Under the encumbered eyelid,
Through the rippled drum of the
             hair-buried ear;

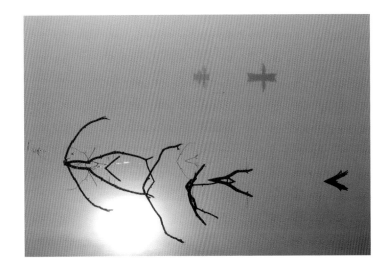

The colossal intimacies of silent
    Once seen strangers or shades on a stair;
There the dark blade and wanton sighing her down
To a haycock couch and the scythes of his arms

...while I've been sitting down trying to write a
poem about a man who fished with a woman
for bait and caught a horrible collection.

The bows glided down, and the coast
Blackened with birds took a last look
At his thrashing hair and whale-blue eye;
The trodden town rang its cobbles for luck.

Sails drank the wind, and white as milk
He sped into the drinking dark;
The sun shipwrecked west on a pearl
And the moon swam out of its hulk

Goodbye, good luck, struck the sun and the moon,
To the fisherman lost on the land.
He stands alone at the door of his home,
With his long-legged heart in his hand.

...a ministerial job is open for a man of the strictest obscurity and intemperance: £1000 a year, excluding tips, bribes, blackmail, blood money, petty cash, and profits realized by the sale of female clerks into the white slave traffic...

O keep his bones away from that common cart,
The morning is flying on the wings of his age
And a hundred storks perch on the sun's right hand.

His golden yesterday asleep upon the iris
And this day's sun leapt up the sky out of her thighs
Was miraculous virginity old as loaves and fishes

...Llangain, near Llanstephan where everyone goes into the pub sideways...and there are more unwanted babies shoved up the chimneys than there are used french letters in the offertory boxes.

We've got a new house... on the Welsh-speaking sea.

And we'll stay in this wood-and-asbestos pagoda
(Till the blackout's raised on London and on me)

A cloud against the glassy sun flutters his
Wings. It would be better if the shutter is shut.
Sinister dark over Cardigan
Bay...It is time for the Black Lion.

Sniff, here is sin! Now he must grapple, rise:
He snuggles deep among the chapel thighs.
And when the moist collection plate is passed
Puts in his penny, generous to the last.

*...such a cold day for walking
abroad, and the wind like a drunk
beggar with his fiddle...*
*time with his winged chariot
hurrying near*

*Back in the bosom, repentant and bloodshot,
Under the draper-sly skies,
I try to forget my week in the mudpot
And cottonwool it in lies.*

*...written down the verse looks a little chaotic-
...heard spoken to a beautiful picture, the words
gain a sense and authority which the printed
word denies them*

It was my thirtieth year to heaven
Woke to my hearing from harbour and neighbour wood
  And the mussel pooled and the heron
      Priested shore

Above the farms and white horses
      And I rose
    In rainy autumn
And walked abroad in a shower of all my days

Forgotten mornings when he walked
            with his mother
  Through the parables
      Of sun light
And the legends of the green chapels

There is no news here: a woman
called Mrs. Prosser died in agony
...I am quite happy and am looking
forward to a gross, obscene and
extremely painful middle-age.

That though I loved them for their faults
As much as for their good,
My friends were enemies on stilts
with their head in a cunning cloud.

A man torn up mourns in the sole night.
And the second comers, the severers, the enemies from
the deep
Forgotten dark, rest their pulse and bury their dead
in her
faithless sleep.

...I have found, increasingly as time
goes on, or around, or backwards, or
stays quite still...that old fear of death,
are as insoluble to me as those of the spirit.

It had been such a ferocious night that someone in the smokey ship-pictured bar had said he could feel his tombstone shaking

The sun lit up the sea town not as a whole- from topmost down - reproving zinc-roofed chapel to empty but for rats and whispers grey warehouse.

The town was not yet awake, and I walked through the streets like a stranger come out of the sea...

I walked past the small sea-spying windows, behind whose trim curtains lay mild-mannered men and women not yet awake...

Smoke from another chimney now. They were burning their last night's dreams. Up from a chimney came a long-haired wraith like an old politician.

The chapel stood grim and grey, telling the day there was to be no nonsense. The chapel was not asleep...

Thus some of the voices of a cliff-perched town at the far end of Wales moved out of sleep and darkness into the new-born, ancient, and ageless morning, moved and were lost.

Now as I was young and easy under the apple
boughs
About the lilting house and happy as the grass
was green,

In the sun that is young once only,
Time let me play and be
Golden in the mercy of his means,

Under the new made clouds and happy as the
heart was long,
In the sun born over and over,
I ran my heedless ways,

Oh as I was young and easy in the mercy of
his means,
Time held me green and dying
Though I sang in my chains like the sea.

*I have a shack at the edge of the cliff where my children
hop like fleas in a box ...and I work among cries and
clatters like a venomous beaver in a parrot house.*

*In this timeless, drizzled, argufying
place...Time has stopped, says the Black Lion
clock and Eternity has begun.*

*When I woke, the town spoke.
Birds and clocks and cross bells
Dinned outside the coiling crowd,*

*Who
Are you
Who is born
In the next room
So loud to my own
That I can hear the womb*

Oh, this Blaencwm room. Fire, pipe, whining, nerves, Sunday joint, wireless, no beer until one in the morning, death. And you aren't here. I think of you all the time, in snow, in bed.

All I shall write in this water and tree room on the cliff, every word, will be my thanks to you... you have given me a life. And now I am going to live it.

'Find meat on bones that soon have none,
And drink in the two milked crags,

The thirst is quenched, the hunger gone,
And my heart is cracked across;
My face is haggard in the glass,
My lips are withered with a kiss,

Fear or believe that the wolf in a sheepwhite hood
Loping and bleating roughly and blithely shall leap,
My dear, my dear,
Out of a lair in the flocked leaves in the dew dipped year
To eat your heart in the house in the rosy wood.

This night and each vast night until the stern bell talks
In the tower and tolls to sleep over the stalls
Of the hearthstone tales my own, last love; and the soul walks
The waters shorn.
This night and each night since the falling star you were born.

Burning ! Night and the vein of birds in the winged, sloe wrist
Of the wood ! Pastoral beat of blood through the laced leaves!
The stream from the priest black wristed spinney and sleeves
Of thistling frost

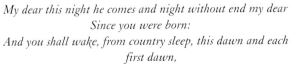

My dear this night he comes and night without end my dear
Since you were born:
And you shall wake, from country sleep, this dawn and each
first dawn,
Your faith as deathless as the outcry of the ruled sun.

Things are appalling here, which can only mean one thing. Bills and demand notes, at me like badgers, whoosh! up the manholes, or gathered, grinning and panting around my bed,

There are rats in the lavatory, tittering while you shit, and the official rat-man comes every day to give them tidbits before the kill.

Before I knocked and flesh let enter,
With liquid hands tapped on the womb,
I who was shapeless as the water

The dream that kicks the buried from
their sack
And lets their trash be honoured as the
quick.
This is the world. Have faith.

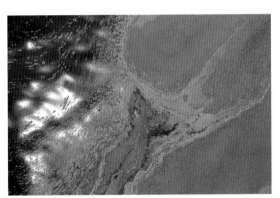

Out of confusion, as the way is,
And the wonder that man knows,
Out of the chaos would come bliss.

...if I am not, before then, popped in the cooler, peeled, pipped
and sliced. I have the skeleton of a story now, but so unpleasant
that it should perhaps remain in its cupboard.

...in his house on stilts high among beaks
And palavers of birds
This sandgrain day in the bent bay's grave

He celebrates and spurns
His driftwood thirty-fifth wind turned age;

Curlews aloud in the congered waves
Work at their ways to death,
And the rhymer in the long tongued room,

Who tolls his birthday bell,
Toils towards the ambush of his words

In his slant, racking house
And the hewn coils of his trade perceives
Herons walk in their shroud

Dark is a way and light is a place,
Heaven that never was
Nor will be ever is always true,

The voyage to ruin I must run,
Dawn ships clouted aground,
Yet though I cry with tumbledown tongue,
Count my blessings aloud;

This day winding down now
At God speeded summer's end
In the torrent salmon sun,

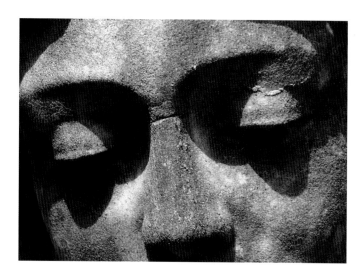

In my seashaken house
On a breakneck of rocks
Tangled with chirrup and fruit,

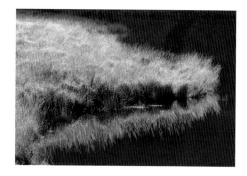

Eternal waters away
From the cities of nine
Days' night whose towers will catch
In the religious wind
Like stalks of tall, dry straw,

Out of these seathumbed leaves
That will fly and fall
Like leaves of trees and as soon
Crumble and undie

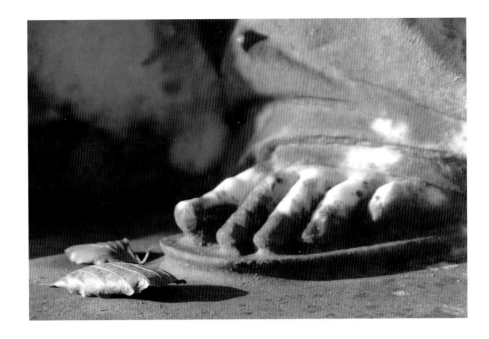

Only the drowned deep bells
Of sheep and churches noise
Poor peace as the sun sets
And dark shoals every holy field.

My ark sings in the sun
At God speeded summer's end
And the flood flowers now.

Over Sir John's hill,
The hawk on fire hangs still;

In a hoisted cloud, at drop of dusk, he pulls to
                                    his claws
And gallows, up the rays of his eyes the small
                              birds of the bay

...To fiery tyburn over the wrestle of elms until
The flash the noosed hawk

Crashes, and slowly the fishing holy stalking
                                    heron
In the river Towy below bows his titled headstone.

I open the leaves of the water at a passage
Of psalms and shadows among the pincered
                    sandcrabs prancing

And read in a shell,
Death clear as a buoy's bell:

It is the heron and I, under judging
                    Sir John's elmed
Hill, tell-tale the knelled

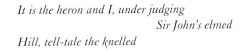

Guilt
Of the led-astray birds whom God, for their
                    breast of whistles,
Have mercy on.

Also I have gout in my toe, phlegm on my lungs, misery in my head, debts in the town, no money in my pocket, and a poem simmering on the hob.

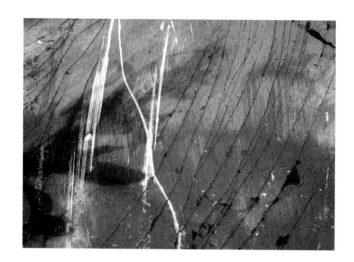

I was sick from the muted, boring thunder of planes in the stratospere...the violent, tentacular intimacies of strangers who forgot one's existence a moment later.

I have a poem nearly finished...if I can, shake off this nervous hag that rides me, biting and scratching into insomnia, nightmare, and the long anxious daylight.

When I was a windy boy and a bit
And the black spit of the chapel fold,
(Sighed the old ram rod, dying of women),

...And on seesaw Sunday nights I wooed
Whoever I would with my wicked eyes,
The whole of the moon I would love and leave.

When I was a gusty man and a half
And the black beast of the beetles' pews,
(Sighed the old ram rod, dying of bitches),

...Wherever I ramped in the clover quilts,
Whatsoever I did in the coal-
Black night, I left my quivering prints.

When I was a man you could call a man
And the black cross of the holy house,
(Sighed the old ram rod, dying of welcome),

...Oh, time enough when the blood creeps cold,
And I lie down but to sleep in bed,
For my sulking, skulking, coal black soul !

When I was a half of the man I was
And serve me right as the preachers warn,
(Sighed the old ram rod, dying of downfall),
No flailing calf or cat in a flame
Or hickory bull in milky grass
But a black sheep with a crumpled horn,

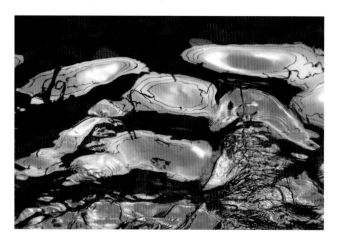

Now I am a man no more no more
And a black reward for a roaring life,
(Sighed the old ram rod, dying of strangers),

Tidy and cursed in my dove cooed room
I lie down thin and hear the good bells jaw-

For, oh, my soul found a sunday wife
In the coal black sky and she bore angels !
Harpies around me out of her womb !
Chastity prays for me, piety sings,
Innocence sweetens my last black breath,
Modesty hides my thighs in her wings,
And all the deadly virtues plague my death !

...go for long walks, healthy as a briar pipe...-and a spring in my step and a song in my gut and poems to write and no need to hurry to write them.

And if you ever manage to visit this country...fish, cockles and mussels, flat warm Welsh bitter beer, affection,

...are all yours...this hymnal blob, this pretty, sick, fond, sad Wales.

The only person I can't show the little enclosed poem to is, of course, my father, who doesn't know he's dying.

*Do not go gentle into that good night,
Old age should burn and rave at the close of day;
Rage, rage against the dying of the light.*

*Though wise men at their end know dark is right,
Because their words had forked no lightning they
Do not go gentle into that good night.*

*...Do not go gentle into that good night
Rage, rage against the dying of the light.*

'llareggub', ...Out of it came the idea that I write a piece, a play, an impression for voices, an entertainment out of the darkness, of the town I live in,

-(the wonderful wish words that sing like thrushes at night, out of the down-at-heel darkness, to the dispossessed in their little black beds) -they all faded.

I do not want to express only what other people have felt; I want to rip something away and show what they have never seen.

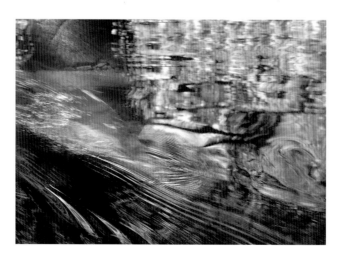

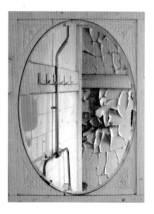

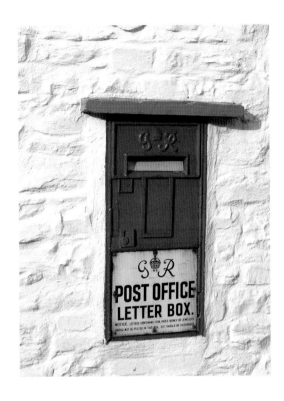

You told me, once, upon a time, to call on you when I was beaten down...

I should with my beggar's cup
Howl down the wind and call your name
And you, would raise me up.

...flew over America like a damp, ranting bird; boomed and fiddled while home was burning; ...you damned Welshcake, for doom'll nibble you down to the last loud crumb ...home again now in this tumbling house whose every broken pane and wind-whipped-off slate, childscrawled wall, rain-stain, mousehole, knobble and ricket man-booby-and-rat-trap

...too many artists of Wales stay in Wales too long, giants in the dark behind the parish pump, pygmies in the nationless sun,

...on my father's death. Poor old boy, he was in awful pain at the end and nearly blind... he said, 'It's a full circle now.'

Time is a foolish fancy, time and fool.
No, no, you lover skull, descending hammer
Descends, my masters, on the entered honour.

Through throats where many rivers meet, the
curlews cry,
Under the conceiving moon, on the high chalk
hill,

And there this night I walk in the
white giant's thigh
Where barren as boulders women
lie longing still

To labour and love though they lay down
long ago.

Through throats where many rivers meet,
the women pray,
Pleading in the waded bay for the seeds
to flow

Though the names on their weed grown stones
are rained away,

Teach me the love that is evergreen after the
fall leaved
Grave, after Beloved on the grass gulfed cross
is scrubbed
Off by the sun and Daughters no longer
grieved

And the daughters of darkness flame like
Fawkes fires still.

*- this is the wet, grey morning, all seabirds
and mist and children's far-off voices and
regret everywhere in the wind and rain,*

*...white owls wheeze in the castle and there
was a fight in the churchyard last night
and I can hear now the cries of the village
idiot being tortured by children in the Square*

*...I talk of going to the States in a very
few weeks...But before I go, I have to clear
up everything here and leave it (almost)
sweet and smiling.*

Yours,

Dylan Thomas

Sept 1953

The photograph is married to the eye,
Grafts on its bride one-sided skins of truth;

The dream has sucked the sleeper of his faith
That shrouded men might marrow as they fly.

For we shall be a shouter like the cock,
Blowing the old dead back; our shots shall smack
The image from the plates;
And we shall be fit fellows for a life,

I fled the earth and, naked, climbed
*   the weather,*
Reaching a second ground far from the
*   stars;*
And there I wept, I and a ghostly other,

Now I am a man no more no more
And a black reward for a roaring life,
(Sighed the old ram rod, dying of strangers).

ARTISTS NOTES

This project started when I was first introduced to Dylan Thomas's amazing ability to create poetic images through his writing. As a visual artist I found that I was actively looking for images that I felt harmonized with those inspired by his words. This soon became an all consuming obsession as I travelled Wales visiting the places he had written about seeking the subject matter that had initially inspired him. I soon realised that these resultant images would fall into three main categories, being dependant on the type of writing under consideration.

1. Descriptive; this is where Dylan was writing about a particular place, perhaps Cwmdonkin Park, or Laugharne. Authenticity, wherever possible, was of prime importance as I searched that area for his inspirations.

2. Illustrative; this applied mainly to his stories where images that helped explain rather than add any extra dimension were required. Again the photographs were taken in the same environment that he wrote about.

3. Thought provoking; certainly the most challenging section. This meant reading his often complex poetry seeking word, line or stanza that created actual visual images in my mind. In many cases there would be a number of possible images within just one line, complicating the process even more. I realised that these should be my own interpretations and not influenced by other opinions as to the meaning behind his writing.

Technical information: All images where taken with either the Fuji S1 or S2 Pro digital camera and a Sigma 28-300 lens. I feel other technical information is unimportant except to say all images were hand-held as I believe in spontaneity in photography comes before careful consideration.

Brian Gaylor FRPS BA(hons)

Image Details:

1 Sunrise over Swansea Bay.
2. View over Uplands to the sea.
3, 4, 5 Across Swansea Bay to the Mumbles.
6. Cwmdonkin Park, Swansea.
7,8,9,10,11,12. Details from Cwmdonkin Park.
13. Reflections in moving water.
15. Old railings Mumbles.
16. Evening, Swansea park.
17. Dry grasses with water behind.
18. Tree shadow.
19. Derelict house.
20. Conifers, Gower.
21. Gnarled tree.
22. Mumbles Head, Swansea.
23. Swansea Docks.
24. Limeslade Bay, Swansea.
25. Mumbles Pier.
26. Old schoolroom, Swansea.
27. Winter park.
28. Mist on pond.
29. Swansea Bay.
30. Ivy grown window.
33. Cwmdonkin Park.
34. Water reflection.
35. The 'Sands', Swansea Bay.
36. Swansea Docks.
37. Broadpool, Gower.
38. Derelict workshop.
39. Seamist, Mumbles Head.
40, 41. Rhosilli Bay, Gower.
41a. Mumbles.
42. Graveyard, Swansea.
43. Graveyard, Swansea Valley.
43/a. Derelict building.
44. Stream bottom.
45,46. Three Cliffs Bay, Gower.
47. Winter Falls, South Wales Coast.
48. Broadpool, Gower.
49. Winter sunset.
50. Derelict workplace.
51. Bible College, Swansea.
52. Gatepost.
53. Airshaft, Nr. Swansea.
54. Old tower, Gower.
55. Burnt house.
56. Conifer Plantation.
57. Tree tunnel, nr Swansea. (Negative).
58. Gower Farmyard.
59. Window detail, St. Pauls, Sketty, Swansea.

60, 61. Old stables, Carmarthenshire.
62 Brambles behind window.
63. Old farm, Carmarthenshire.
64. A dingle near Carmarthen.
65. Oystermouth Cemetery, Swansea.
66,67 Swansea Valley.
68. Autumn Beech leaves.
69. Abandoned doll.
70. Clyne Gardens, Swansea.
71. Laugharne window.
72,73,74,75,76,77. Swansea Docks.
78,79,80. Singleton Park, Swansea.
81. Old hospital bench, Swansea.
82. Winter river, Carmarthenshire.
83,84,85. War memorials, Swansea.
86. Beach at Llanrhidian, Gower.
87. Welsh chapel, Swansea Valley.
88. Reflections in pond.
89. Dead sheep.
90. Burnt chapel, Swansea.
91. Detail, dead tree.
92. Broken mirror.
93. Swansea Docks.
94. Frozen log in waterfall.
95. Derelict washroom, Bible College, Swansea.
96. Winter track, Swansea Valley.
97. Old schoolroom, Carmarthenshire.
98. Bible College, Swansea.
99. Porthole, Swansea Docks.
100. Oystermouth Cemetery.
101. Across Swansea Bay to Mumbles Head.
102. Overgrown shelter, Carmarthenshire.
103. Flaking paint.
104. Derelict house.
105. Grave detail, Carmarthenshire.
106. Shadows.
107. Reflections.
108. Pews, Welsh chapel, Swansea.
109. Ruined cottage, Swansea Valley.
110. Shadows.
111.. Church, near Swansea.
112. Old Manor house, near Swansea.
113. Peeling paint.
114. Reflections.
115. Brambles behind glass.
116. Carmarthenshire, cemetery
117. Dead trees, near Swansea.
118,119,120. Oystermouth Cemetery
121. Rhosilli Bay, Gower.
122. Coast detail, near Swansea.

123,124. Caswell Bay, Gower.
125,126,127. Details, Swansea.
128. Disused Church, Carmarthenshire.
129. St Pauls, Sketty, Swansea.
130. Paintbrush wipes.
131. Cracked paint on door.
132. Lady's bow.
133. Cave entrance, Carmarthenshire.
134. Sheep remains.
135. Black Mountain, Carmarthenshire.
136. Mountain road, near Swansea.
137. Sunken wall, Swansea Valley.
138. Ferns.
138/a Church window detail.
139. Hill farm, Swansea Valley.
140. Hearth, derelict cottage.
141. Peeling paint.
142. Carmarthenshire countryside.
143 Winter Quince.
144. Forest mist.
145. Grave railings.
146. Gower from Laugharne.
147. Hedgrow, Swansea Valley.
148. Sand patterns.
149, 150. Carmarthenshire countryside.
151,152,153. Derelict house.
154. St. Martins, Laugharne.
155. Burnt chapel, Swansea.
156. Skull.
157. Conifers.
158. Derelict house, Carmarthenshire.
159. Old cottage, South Wales.
161. Disused interior.
161/a. Roofscape, Swansea.
162. Dylan's Bedroom, 5 Cwmdonkin Drive.
163. Mask.
164. Sunken doll's head.
165. 'Seaview', Laugharne.
166. Frozen reeds, Carmarthenshire.
167. Frost, Swansea Valley.
168. Storm clouds.
169. Winter estuary, Laugharne.
170 Winter conifers.
171. Winter, Swansea Valley.
172. Barbed-wire.
173. Roosting crows, winter.
174. Church memorial, Carmarthenshire.
175. Winter morning, Carmarthenshire.
176. Carmarthen.
177 Penrice Church, Gower.